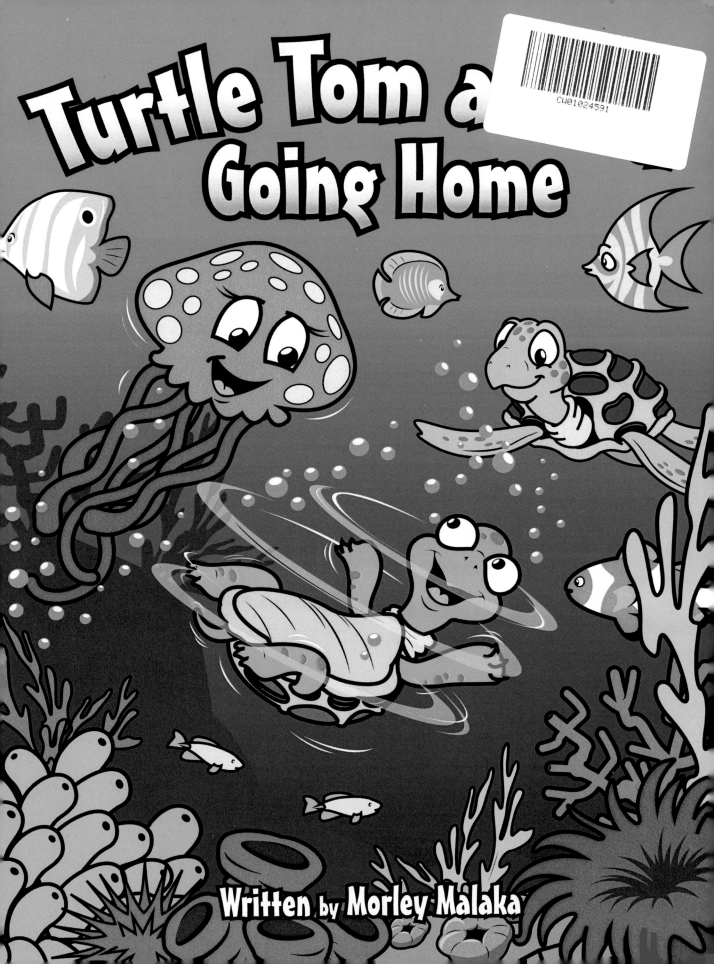

Turtle Tom a
Going Home

Written by Morley Malaka

ISBN-10: 1514863073
ISBN-13: 978-1514863077

Going Home

The last time we saw Turtle Tom, he had managed to get himself dumped near a beach. There he met some new and unusual creatures. Without warning, Tom was washed up from the beach and into the sea. It happened so fast that he barely had any time to react. He was splashing around and trying to figure out how to survive the tides that stole him.

Suddenly, Tom was scooped up by a quick hawk with an amazing set of wings and claws. Here we go again, he thought to himself. Turtle Tom was on another adventure. Where could the hawk be taking him?

Turtle Tom realizes that the hawk is carrying him higher and higher into the sky. *We're going to the moon?* Turtle Tom thought. Just then, he begins to slip out of the Hawk's grip, and just like that, Tom is headed back to the water. *Whoaaaaaa!*

As Tom plunges into the sea, he realizes that he is able to breathe underwater just fine. As a matter of fact, he feels like he was born to swim. *Wow, this should make finding my family much easier,* he thinks.

Soon after, Tom sees a colorful creature slowly making her way towards him. She is so beautiful and has really long legs. In fact, she has lots of long legs. She is a jellyfish and her name is Rissa.

She swims up to Tom and wiggles all of her legs at him. *Rissa is definitely not a family member of mine but what a great swimmer she is,* thought Turtle Tom. The little turtle is happy to have met a new friend.

The two of them playfully imitate each other as they swim around. Just then, a huge whale swims by and Tom remembers that he is on a mission to find his family.

7

Tom sees a bunch of shrimp near the bottom of the sea. They have whiskers and long bodies. *They are very strange looking creatures*, Tom thinks. The shrimp begin to scurry away when they see Tom looking at them. Turtle Tom does not understand why.

Swimming along they see lots of other sea creatures. There are big fish and little fish, round fish and sword fish. There are so many fish to see, but none of these are the turtle's family.

Some of the fish are swimming alone while others are in a big group. *Those fish must be a family,* thinks Tom. He watches as the fish swim together.

11

Then, Turtle Tom catches a glimpse of something in the distance. It is moving toward him very slowly. Tom is not sure what to make of it. Turtle Tom decides to swim closer to get a better look.

All of a sudden, Tom is face to face with another turtle. He is shocked at how big this other turtle is. *What an amazing creature*, Turtle Tom thinks.

13

All of a sudden, Tom feels something closing in on him. What can it be? Oh no! A net is trapping Turtle Tom. Yet, Tom is not alone. There are fish tangled in the net with him.

Tom realizes that the other turtle is not in the net. He sees the large turtle tugging on the rope. However, the large turtle is not strong enough to set Tom free. He watches, in horror, as Turtle Tom is lifted above the surface of the sea.

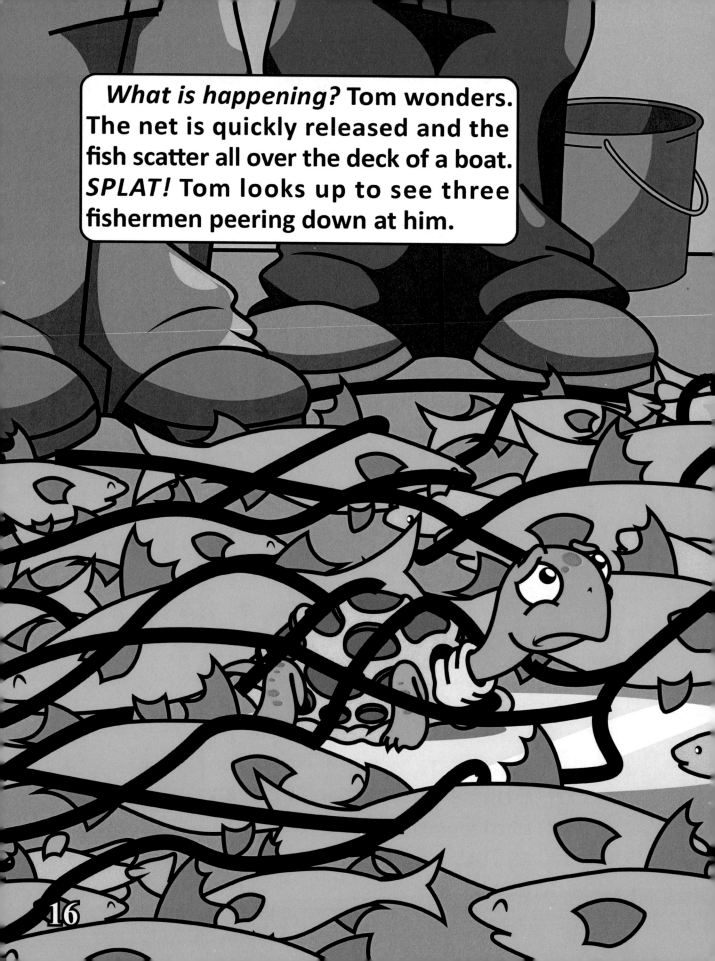

"Look what we have here," says one of the fishermen. "It's a sea turtle," says the other. Turtle Tom is scared. He wants to get away, but the net still has him pinned.

17

"Let's make turtle soup out of him!" says one of the men as he licks his lips. Turtle Tom is sad and unsure of what to do. He had finally found another turtle but now his adventure seems to be over.

Just then, another fisherman comes up to them. He looks at the turtle and smiles kindly. "Wait a minute fellas," he says. "This here is a baby turtle. We might as well put him back in the water." Then he takes Turtle Tom and leans over the boat. "Be free turtle! Swim away!" says the fisherman.

Within moments, Turtle Tom is back in the sea. He is quickly reunited with Rissa and the big turtle. The big turtle is very excited to see that Tom is free.

Tom is overjoyed to finally be at home with another turtle. The big turtle cannot wait to show the little turtle around. However, he is especially excited to introduce Tom to his family.

23

Together Turtle Tom, Rissa, and the big turtle swim deeper and deeper into the sea, until their shadows can be seen no more.

What a tremendous journey it has been for Turtle Tom. He has been on many adventures and met a lot of friends. From the woods, to the farm, to school, through the city, to the zoo, to the beach and now at home in the sea.

The Adventures of Turtle Tom is aimed at making everyone a believer. It is a story of challenges, fun, setbacks and excitement; but most importantly, of hope. Turtle Tom never gave up on finding his family and doesn't ever want you to give up on your journey too.

THE END

FUN FACT

Turtles are cold blooded animals, they belong to the reptile family.

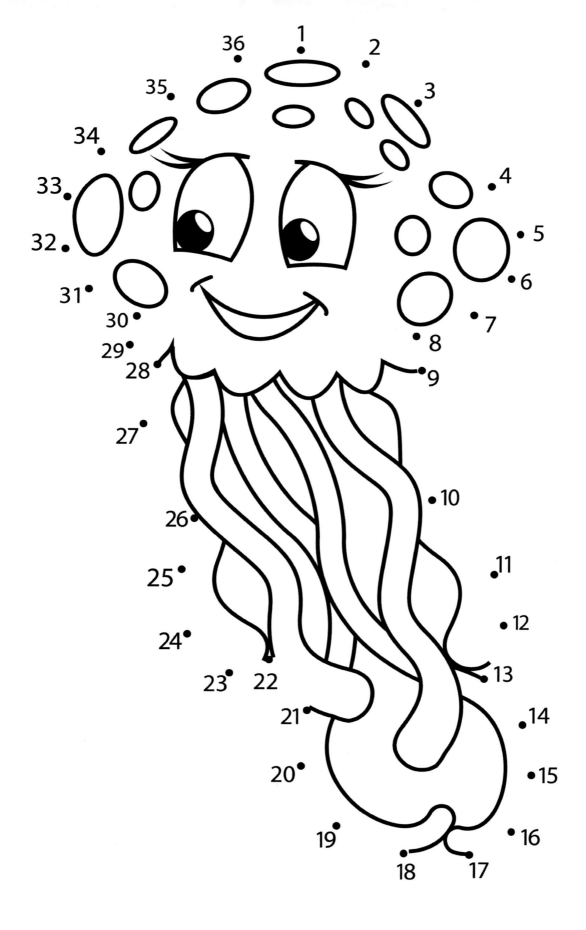

The End!

https://www.amazon.com/author/morleymalaka
www.turtletombooks.com
www.facebook.com/turtletombooks

Made in the USA
Middletown, DE
23 November 2015